BIG IDEA'S VeggieTales

The Ballad of LITTLE JOE

Adapted by Karen Poth
Illustrated by Paul Conrad

Based on the VeggieTales® video *The Ballad of Little Joe*

A GOLDEN BOOK • NEW YORK

Published in the United States by Golden Books, an imprint of Random House Children's Books, a division of Random House, Inc., 1745 Broadway, New York, NY 10019, and in Canada by Random House of Canada Limited, Toronto. Originally published as a Little Golden Treasure under the title *The Ballad of Little Joe* in 2007. Golden Books, A Golden Book, A Little Golden Book, Little Golden Treasures, the G colophon, and the distinctive gold spine are registered trademarks of Random House, Inc.
www.randomhouse.com/kids
Library of Congress Control Number: 2008930602   ISBN: 978-0-375-85144-5
Printed in the United States of America
10 9 8 7 6 5 4
First Edition

A long, long time ago, way out West, lived twelve cowboy brothers. Their names were Reuben, Simeon, Levi, Izzy, Zeb, Gad, Ash, Dan, Natty, and Jude. There was also Baby Ben. But he was too little to go outside. Oh, and there was one more—Little Joe.

Now, Little Joe was different from all his brothers. For one thing, he was a lot taller. And he didn't have a French accent.

But more troubling to his brothers was that
Little Joe was their father's favorite son.

On Little Joe's birthday, his father gave him a beautiful Western vest.

His brothers, who all got mittens for their birthdays, didn't like that one doggone bit. And that was when Little Joe headed into all sorts of trouble!

His brothers were so jealous, they tossed him into an old mine shaft!

"HEY, JUDE!" Little Joe called out to his big brother from the darkness of the mine.

But Jude didn't help. Instead, he sold Little Joe to a band of desperados. That's Western talk for robbers.

Well, those robbers took Little Joe to Dodge Ball City. There they sold him to the owner of the Rootin' Tootin' Pizza Place.

From that day on, Little
Joe worked hard selling
pizza and root beer.

But that didn't get Little Joe down. He made a bunch of friends, and after a year, he was named employee of the month!

Unfortunately, that made Miss Kitty, the waitress, burning mad. Miss Kitty was so jealous that she had Little Joe thrown in jail.

"Little Joe, why is all this bad stuff happening to you?"
asked Sheriff Bob.

"Shucks! I don't really know. But God is good," Little Joe
answered. "I reckon I just have to keep on doin' what's right."

One day, during an important town meeting, the mayor of Dodge Ball City had a dream. It upset him so much that he asked Little Joe to tell him what it meant. And with God's help, Little Joe did just that.

According to the dream, Dodge Ball City would have seven years of plenty—more food than they could ever eat. Then they would have seven years of severe famine—no pizza and no root beer!

To thank Little Joe for his help, the mayor made him the second most powerful man in Dodge Ball City.

Little Joe got to work right away preparing the town for the hard days to come. During the seven good years, the city stored up plenty of food.

Then, just as Little Joe had said, the bad years of famine came. The people of Dodge Ball City were fine . . . thanks to Little Joe. But Little Joe's family had just one pancake to share. They were doomed!

So all eleven of Little Joe's brothers and his father
traveled to Dodge Ball City in search of food.

When Little Joe saw them coming, he wasn't sure he could trust his brothers. So he greeted them wearing a tricky disguise.

But Little Joe's brothers hadn't come to Dodge Ball City to cause trouble. They needed help for themselves and for their father.

"We would like to buy some food from you," Jude told Little Joe.

Little Joe soon realized how God had used all the bad things that had happened to him for good. Thanks to the hardships he had endured, he could now help his family.

Little Joe forgave his brothers, and they had the best family reunion the West had ever seen!

YEE-HA!